# HYPNO-SEXUALITY

## ERICH KASSLER

www.dizzyemupublishing.com

DIZZY EMU PUBLISHING
1714 N McCadden Place, Hollywood, Los Angeles 90028
www.dizzyemupublishing.com

**Hypno-Sexuality**
Erich Kassler

ISBN: 9798559470597

First published in the United States
in 2020 by Dizzy Emu Publishing

www.dizzyemupublishing.com

# HYPNO-SEXUALITY

ERICH KASSLER

# HYPNO-SEXUALITY

## An Erotic Screenplay

### By

### Erich Kassler
### (Copyright 2020 By The Author)

## THE CAST (In Order Of Appearance)

DR. ZIGMOND--------------------------------Famous Hypno-Sexologist
MARY-JANE, aka   JEANETTE-MARIE------------A Beautiful Patient
VANESSA TALBOT----------------------A Beautiful Magazine Reporter
HEATHER---------------------------------------------The Doctor's Secretary
LISA, aka APHRODITE----------------------Another Beautiful Patient
JERRY----------------------------------------------------------A Male Patient
BRENT-------------------------------------------------Another Male Patient
LACEY LOVING----------------------------------------------------A Porn Star
REBECCA DEE-------------------------------------------Another Porn Star
HENRY STYLES------------------------------------------A Porn Director
ERNIE----------------------------------------------------HENRY'S Assistant

INTERIOR–TREATMENT ROOM ONE–DAY

(Fade In on the image of a hypnotic spiral that spins around as the opening credits fade in and out over it. The camera then pulls back and we see that the spiral is an image on a TV screen. Cut To a shot of the room with DR. ZIGMOND sitting on a chair next to MARY-JANE, who sits upon a long chaise lounge staring at the TV screen. DR. ZIGMOND is an older, handsome, professional-looking man with a slightly sleazy gleam in his eye.   He wears a white lab coat over a shirt and tie and suit pants.   MARY-JANE is a gorgeous young woman dressed in a black slit skirt, fish-net stockings, a tight top with horizontal black-and-white stripes, a red scarf tied around her neck, and a red berét–if she were dressed anymore stereotypically French, she'd be wearing a maid's outfit. DR. ZIGMOND speaks to her as she sits, fascinated by the spiral image.)

             DR. ZIGMOND
Concentrate on the spinning spiral---Let it become the only thing you see—and as you focus all your attention on the spinning spiral—focus all your attention on the spinning spiral—you feel yourself become more and more relaxed---more and more relaxed---more and more relaxed—

(Cut To an image of the hypnotic spiral as it turns. Cut To a Close-Up of MARY-JANE as she stares at the spiral Off-Camera, eyes blinking sleepily, getting heavy as DR. ZIGMOND continues talking.)

             DR. ZIGMOND
Let your mind and your body become more and more relaxed---more and more relaxed---more and more relaxed—Your eyes feel so very heavy—so very, very, heavy—you can barely keep them open as you become more and more relaxed---more and more relaxed---more and more relaxed—it feels so very good to relax—to just let yourself drift away into nothingness—to just let your mind go completely blank—to let your eyes close---let your eyes close—as you become deeply and completely relaxed---deeply and completely relaxed---deeply and completely relaxed—

(MARY-JANE closes her eyes and relaxes completely. DR. ZIGMOND lifts up one of her hands, sees that it is completely limp, then lets it fall back into her lap.)

             DR. ZIGMOND
Listen to me very carefully, Mary-Jane. You are in a state of deep, wonderful relaxation—a trance, actually.   Oh, let's be honest about it—you are hypnotized.   Say it.

             MARY-JANE
(In a soft, sleepy monotone) I am hypnotized.

             DR. ZIGMOND
Very good. Now, listen very carefully. In a moment I will say to you, "Open your eyes." The next time you hear those words you will open your eyes, but you will still be deeply hypnotized. You will focus your attention on the spinning spiral and listen intently

to every suggestion I give you. Do you understand, Mary-Jane?

                    MARY-JANE
Yes, Dr. Zigmond. I understand.

                    DR. ZIGMOND
Good.   And now—open your eyes.

(MARY-JANE opens her eyes and continues staring into the hypnotic spiral on the TV screen. Cut To the image of the hypnotic spiral. Cut To DR. ZIGMOND and MARY-JANE.)

                    DR. ZIGMOND
With each turn of the spinning spiral you become more deeply and completely hypnotized.   The more deeply and completely hypnotized you become, the more receptive you become to my suggestions—the more willing you become to follow my commands.   Do you understand?

                    MARY-JANE
Yes, Dr. Zigmond.   I understand.

                    DR. ZIGMOND
Excellent.   You're very good at being hypnotized.   Now—the reason you came to me to be hypnotized was that you wished to more greatly enjoy the pleasures of fellatio.   Quite frankly, you made the right choice–hypnosis is the best way to open up your mind, smash your inhibitions senseless, and enable you to become the hot, sexy, swinging cocksucker that we both know you can be—that we both know you want to be—that makes a man stand up, salute, and say, "By golly, I'm glad I have a dick so I can get it sucked by a hot, sexy, swinging cocksucker!"

(As he says the line, DR. ZIGMOND becomes more and more exuberant as he really gets into the idea of turning MARY-JANE into a hot, sexy, swinging cocksucker, so that he's almost shouting at the end.   He collects himself, though, and quiets down, looking at MARY-JANE to make sure she didn't awaken.   Not to worry—she's still hypnotized and staring at the TV screen.)

                    DR. ZIGMOND
(Subdued) Emmm–do you understand?

                    MARY-JANE
Yes, Dr. Zigmond.   I understand.

                    DR. ZIGMOND
Glorious.   Now—in order for you to fully embrace and comprehend the intricacies and mysteries of all things oral, you must understand that few, if any, are better at oral sex than the French.   That is why it's called French love, after all.   And so, in

order for you to understand French love, you must become, in your hypnotized mind—French. Do you understand?

                    MARY-JANE
Yes, Dr. Zigmond   I understand.


                    DR. ZIGMOND
Superb. Now—you are about to become, in your hypnotized mind, the French woman Jeanette-Marie.   Jeanette-Marie is a beautiful woman, a thoroughly sexual woman, who loves sex in all its forms—especially oral sex. Jeanette-Marie loves nothing more than to take a man's cock and make hot, delicious French love to it with her mouth and tongue.   And you, my dear, are Jeanette-Marie—you are that hot delicious piece of French pastry who loves to suck cock with a French accent.   Do you understand?


                    MARY-JANE
Yes, Dr. Zigmond.   I understand.


                    DR. ZIGMOND
(Smiling triumphantly) Magnificent! Now I want you to repeat after me–and you will repeat after me–"When I hear the count of three—I will become Jeanette-Marie."


                    MARY-JANE
When I hear the count of three—I will become Jeanette-Marie.


                    DR. ZIGMOND
Say it again.


                    MARY-JANE
When I hear the count of three—I will become Jeanette-Marie.


                    DR. ZIGMOND
Now say those words twenty times over, and with each time you repeat the phrase, you will drift twenty times deeper into deep hypnosis.   And I'll be back to check upon your progress.


                    (DR. ZIGMOND exits the room, and the camera focuses on MARY-JANE as she sits in trance, staring at the screen and repeating the phrase.)


                    MARY-JANE
When I hear the count of three—I will become Jeancttc-Marie---When I hear the count of three—I will become Jeanette-Marie---When I hear the count of three—I will become Jeanette-Marie—


          (Cut To–)

INTERIOR–OFFICE LOBBY–DAY

(As the doctor's gorgeous secretary HEATHER sits at her desk doing secretarial things, the beautiful magazine reporter VANESSA TALBOT, dressed in a short-skirted business suit that clings tastefully to her curvy frame, enters ths scene from Camera Right.   She stops and stands before HEATHER'S desk, almost posing before it. HEATHER looks up at her.)

           HEATHER
May I help you?

           VANESSA
Yes—I'm Vanessa Talbot, from Sexuality Today magazine. I'm here to interview Dr. Zigmond about his use of hypnosis in helping people with their enjoyment of sex. I believe we spoke on the phone—are you Heather?

           HEATHER
Yes, I'm Dr. Zigmond's secretary.   The Doctor has a fairly full schedule today, but I'm sure he'll have time for you. If you'll please have a seat, I'll let him know you're here.

(As VANESSA takes a seat, HEATHER picks up the phone and pushes the intercom button.)

           HEATHER
(To the phone) Dr. Zigmond?   Vanessa Talbot from Sexuality Today is here for your interview. (Pause) All right, I'll let her know. You're welcome.

(HEATHER hangs up and speaks to VANESSA.)

           HEATHER
He says he'll be with you shortly.

           VANESSA
While I'm waiting, could I ask you a few questions?

           HEATHER
Certainly.

           VANESSA
I've noticed in my research that the majority of the Doctor's patients are beautiful women. Is there a particular reason for that?

           HEATHER
Well, he does have his male patients, too.

                    VANESSA
Yes, I know, but not as many as he does female patients.

                    HEATHER
Well—the doctor does have a special rapport with women,

                    VANESSA
(Very skeptical) Special rapport?

                    HEATHER
Yes. And because he has this rapport, women trust him and realize he wants to
help them. It's as simple as that.

                    VANESSA
Has he ever used this special rapport on you?

                    HEATHER
Ms. Talbot, I'm not a patient of his. I'm his secretary.

(Cut To VANESSA, still looking skeptical. Cut To---)

INTERIOR---TREATMENT ROOM TWO—DAY

(LISA, a gorgeous, busty woman with a gorgeous head of long, full hair, sits on a
love seat waiting for DR. ZIGMOND. She wears a flowing white Greek-style toga that
leaves one gorgeous shoulder bare. DR. ZIGMOND enters from Camera Left and LISA
stands up to greet him.)

                    DR. ZIGMOND
Hello, Lisa—are we ready to begin?

                    LISA
Well, yes—I suppose—but you still haven't explained why you had me put on
this toga.

                    DR. ZIGMOND
That will become evident when you see yourself—in the mirror—

(As he says the line, DR. ZIGMOND pulls a vanity mirror out of his lab coat and
holds it up to LISA.   She sees her reflection and is immediately fascinated.   Her hands
slowly drop to her sides and her breathing deepens, her bust rising and falling with every
breath.)

                    DR. ZIGMOND
That's it—stare into your own eyes, just like you've done before—stare into your
own eyes, and become captivated—fascinated—entranced—hypnotized—

LISA
(Soft and dreamy) Hypnotized—

DR. ZIGMOND
You are hypnotized. Say it.

LISA
I am hypnotized.

DR, ZIGMOND
You are completely receptive to all of my suggestions.

LISA
I am completely receptive to all of your suggestions.

DR. ZIGMOND
You're doing very well—now, take the mirror in your hand, and have a seat.

(LISA takes the mirror by the handle and sits down, never once taking her eyes off her reflection. DR. ZIGMOND sits down beside her; she doesn't even notice.)

DR. ZIGMOND
Now—you came to me because you wanted to be able to enjoy anal sex, to become receptive to the idea of a man's cock thrusting and driving up your behind. Considering this carefully, is this still what you want?

LISA
Yes, Dr, Zigmond.

DR. ZIGMOND
Very well, then—in order for you to understand anal sex, you must understand that no one understands anal sex better than the Greeks.   The Greeks invented butt-humping–they live it, they love it, they taught the world how to do the backdoor bongo.   And for you to learn to do the backdoor bongo, you must let yourself become Greek.   Do you accept this suggestion into your hypnotized mind, Lisa?

LISA
(Pause) Yes, Dr, Zigmond.

DR. ZIGMOND
Beautiful.   Now, as you let yourself become a Greek lover, accept that you are becoming not just any Greek lover—you are becoming the most famous Greek lover of all time—you are becoming Aphrodite, the Greek goddess of love and beauty.   Let yourself feel the transformation in your hypnotized mind and beautiful body, as you become the goddess of love.

(LISA straightens up in her seat and arches her back. Completely engrossed in her own reflection, she gently caresses her face and brushes her hair with her free hand. Not once in the scene does she stop staring in the mirror.)

DR. ZIGMOND
As Aphrodite, you love and adore all things sexual, and no one is better at sex than the goddess of love.   Just the thought of sex—any kind of sex—makes you instantly and passionately aroused, and when Aphrodite is aroused, the whole world becomes aroused.   And when Aphrodite takes it in her mouth—in her pussy—and especially in her ass—the whole world rejoices!   And when Aphrodite has multiple, rapid-fire orgasms—and she always has multiple, rapid-fire orgasms—the whole world cums screaming!   Isn't that wonderful?

LISA
(Smiling) It certainly is!

DR. ZIGMOND
Then answer me–who are you becoming?

LISA
(Breathless and passionate) I am becoming Aphrodite, the goddess of love.

DR. ZIGMOND
Marvelous!   Now, in a moment, you will hear a voice counting from one to three. And when you hear the count of three, at that point the process of transformation will be complete, and you will become Aphrodite, the goddess with a passion for all things sexual—especially Greek sex.   Do you understand?

LISA
(Again, breathless and passionate) Oh, yes—yes.

DR. ZIGMOND
Then repeat after me—"When I hear the count of three—I will completely be—Aphrodite."

LISA
When I hear the count of three—I will completely be—Aphrodite.

DR. ZIGMOND
Say that again.

LISA
When I hear the count of three—I will completely be—Aphrodite.

DR. ZIGMOND
Perfect. Now you repeat that over and over in your hypnotized mind—and I'll be back with you shortly.

(DR. ZIGMOND stands up and exits the scene, leaving LISA staring hypnotized into the mirror, admiring her reflection. Cut To—)

INTERIOR–OFFICE LOBBY—DAY

(DR. ZIGMOND enters the lobby, and HEATHER and VANESSA stand up to greet him.)

HEATHER
Dr. Zigmond, may I present Vanessa Talbot, from Sexuality Today magazine. Ms. Talbot, this is Dr. Zigmond.

VANESSA
How do you do, Doctor.

DR. ZIGMOND
I'm doing quite well, Ms. Talbot. And yourself?

VANESSA
The same.

DR. ZIGMOND
Excellent. I have two gentlemen patients I need to see, but my secretary will show you into my office, and I'll be with you momentarily. Will that be satisfactory?

VANESSA
Certainly.

DR. ZIGMOND
(Smiling) All right.   I'll see you shortly.

(DR. ZIGMOND exits the lobby, leaving HEATHER and VANESSA alone)

HEATHER
You see? I told you he had male patients.

(VANESSA shrugs in lieu of saying "whatever," and follows HEATHER as the exit the scene for DR. ZIGMOND'S office. Cut To—)

INTERIOR—TREATMENT ROOM THREE—DAY

(DR. ZIGMOND enters the room to find JERRY, a moderately handsome man sitting in a comfortable chair, whimpering with his head in his hands. He barely notices as DR. ZIGMOND takes a seat in front of him, and he watches for a moment as a grief-stricken JERRY appears to be on the verge of collapse.)

DR. ZIGMOND
Can you–can you tell me how I can help you, my friend?

JERRY
(Whimpering) It's—I don't know what to do. I haven't been able to get it up in months.

DR. ZIGMOND
I could see why that could distress you—

JERRY
You can't!  No one can. When I think about all the men my wife has been with on a weekly basis—sucking them and fucking them, sometimes three or four at a time--I just can't keep her satisfied, no matter how hard I try.  It's like my dick has given up.

DR. ZIGMOND
Your wife—is she a porn star?  An escort?

JERRY
She's a Washington lobbyist.

DR. ZIGMOND
(Taken aback) Oh, dear.

JERRY
I just want to have an erection again. I want to remember what it was like to be happy.

DR. ZIGMOND
I believe I can help you. If you will go down the hall to treatment room one---the door is clearly marked—you will find in there an associate of mine, who will help you to regain your happiness.

JERRY
Do you–do you think so?

DR. ZIGMOND
I can almost guarantee it. (Pause) Almost. Just go in the room and count to three out loud. Then just let things take their course.

(DR. ZIGMOND stands up, and helps JERRY to his feet.  DR. ZIGMOND opens the door, and with a gentle push on his shoulder, sends JERRY down the hall, then exits the room on the opposite direction.  Cut To—)

INTERIOR—TREATMENT ROOM FOUR—DAY

(BRENT, another handsome man, paces the room impatiently.  DR. ZIGMOND enters the room and closes the door behind him. BRENT stops and stares at him expectantly.)

DR. ZIGMOND
Brent, isn't it?  What can I do to help you today?

BRENT
I guess—I guess it would be just as easy to show you.

(BRENT drops his pants to reveal a large and fully erect cock.  DR. ZIGMOND jumps back in surprise.)

DR. ZIGMOND
Whoa! You want to point that thing elsewhere, cowboy?

BRENT
It's been like this for six days, Doctor!  Six days!  I can barely zip my trousers, every woman where I work wants to sue me for sexual harassment—and do you know how to hard it is to take a leak with this thing?

DR. ZIGMOND
Yes—well, that's what you get for buying Viagra over the internet.

BRENT
I'm at my wits' end, Doctor!  You gotta help me!

DR. ZIGMOND
It's quite obvious to me that you need to relieve your stress.  Tell you what—if you will go down to treatment room two—it's right down the hall, you can't miss it—an associate of mine will attend to your needs.

BRENT
You're sure about that?

DR. ZIGMOND
It's certainly a possibility. Just count to three out loud, and go with the flow.

BRENT
All right.  Thank you, Doctor.

(DR. ZIGMOND opens the door, and BRENT pulls up his pants and exits down the hallway.   DR. ZIGMOND follows him out.   Cut To—)

INTERIOR–TREATMENT ROOM ONE–DAY

(JERRY enters the room to see MARY-JANE still sitting and staring at the hypnotic spiral image.   JERRY goes over to her, wondering what's going on. He looks at the TV screen, then back at her.)

            JERRY
Uh—one, two, three?

(MARY-JANE'S eyes flutter, and she comes to her senses—except she's now the hot, sexy French tart JEANETTE-MARIE.   She looks up at JERRY and smiles, then stands up to greet him.)

            JEANETTE-MARIE
(With French accent) Bonjour, monsieur!   Je m'appelle Jeanette-Marie—vous-vous applez-vous?

            JERRY
What?   What did you say?

            JEANETTE-MARIE
Your name, zilly boy—what eez your name?

            JERRY
I'm—I'm Jerry.

            JEANETTE-MARIE
Ooooh, Jerry.   Rhymes with "Cherie."   Oui?

(She rubs up against him in overt flirtation.)

            JERRY
I—I guess so—

            JEANETTE-MARIE
Zo, Jerry—Parlez-vous francais?

            JERRY
No, I only had a year of Spanish in high school.

            JEANETTE-MARIE
Eet eez—how you say—okay?   I can parlez-vous tres magnifiquely.   Let me show you how I parlez-vous—

(JEANETTE-MARIE sits down on the lounge, placing her face at crotch-level with JERRY. She pulls down his pants and sucks and licks his cock, and before long JERRY has a full, glorious erection. Cut To—)

INTERIOR–TREATMENT ROOM TWO–DAY

(BRENT enters the room, closing the door behind him.  He sees LISA sitting in deep trance, still staring into the mirror, motionless as a statue. BRENT stares at her, wondering what is going on.)

           BRENT
One—two—three?

(Upon hearing the count of three, LISA becomes aware of BRENT—only now she's APHRODITE, goddess of love.   She sets down the mirror, then stands up and arches her back to point her bust at him. There is a regal manner to her actions as she glides across the room to stand next to him, putting her hands on his chest with gentle caresses.  BRENT drops his pants in surprise, and his naked cock pops out at her.)

           BRENT
Who are—what are you?

           APHRODITE
I am Aphrodite, goddess of love—

(She suddenly grabs the front of his shirt and pulls him towards her.)

           APHRODITE
(More insistent)—And I want you to fuck my ass!

(We then Cut back and forth between the two scenes as JEANETTE-MARIE has her way playfully and adoringly with JERRY, and APHRODITE has her way lovingly, yet insistently, with BRENT.  The hypnotized women fuck their way through all sorts of positions with their partners rising to the occasion, losing all their clothes in the process—except for JEANETTE-MARIE, who manages to keep her berét on throughout. Towards the climax, we have APHRODITE on her hands and knees on the floor, while BRENT, at her urging, services her anally.)

           APHRODITE
Fuck my ass!

           BRENT
Yes, my goddess!

                    APHRODITE
I said fuck my ass!

                    BRENT
Yes, my goddess!

                    APHRODITE
Fuck it!   Fuck it harder!

          (The fucking continues until JEANETTE-MARIE takes JERRY'S load into her
mouth, swallowing as much as she can.   Cut To APHRODITE pulling BRENT'S cock
out of her ass to take his money shot on her face and breasts.   Cut To—)

INTERIOR—TREATMENT ROOM ONE—DAY

          (JERRY lies on his back on the chaise lounge, exhausted but happy.
JEANETTE-MARIE gets her face out of her crotch and slides up his body to look him in
the eye.)

                    JERRY
At last—I got laid.   I can walk in the sun again.

                    JEANETTE-MARIE
Zo, mon cherie—now can you parlez-vous?

                    JERRY
Oui, oui, Jeanette-Marie–oui, oui.

          (JEANETTE-MARIE smiles contentedly and lays her head on JERRY"S chest.
Cut To–)

INTERIOR—TREATMENT ROOM TWO—DAY

          (BRENT and APHRODITE sit on the love seat together—BRENT, exhausted but
happily relieved, contemplates his now-flaccid dick.   APHRODITE sits facing him,
holding her breasts up as she fondles and displays them for him.)

                    BRENT
Oh, man—I didn't think that was ever going down.

                    APHRODITE
You have served your goddess well—now, how may your goddess serve you?

                    BRENT
Just keep doing what you're doing, and you'll serve me just fine.

(APHRODITE smiles and continues fondling herself, while BRENT breathes several deep sighs of relief.   Dissolve To—)

INTERIOR—DR. ZIGMOND'S OFFICE---DAY

(DR. ZIGMOND sits at his desk with his feet upon it and stares into space as he answers VANESSA'S questions like he's casually chatting about the weather. VANESSA sits in a chair in front of the desk with her legs crossed, taking notes and trying not to look too incredulous. In addition to the desk and chairs, a long comfortable sofa can be seen in the background.)

            DR. ZIGMOND
Now modesty, of course, prohibits me from comparing my humble efforts to such minor luminaries as Albert Kinsey or Masters and Johnson, but in my own quiet and extraordinary way, I've managed to make my own indelible, earth-shaking and revolutionary contributions to the field of human sexuality.

            VANESSA
Alfred.

            DR. ZIGMOND
(Looks at VANESSA)Hmm?

            VANESSA
Kinsey's name wasn't Albert, it was Alfred.

            DR. ZIGMOND
Oh? Yes, well---I hope my modesty wasn't too much of an obstacle in accurately assessing my achievements, Ms. Talbot.

            VANESSA
(Sarcastically) Doctor, you're about as modest as a burlesque dancer.

            DR. ZIGMOND
(Ignores the insult) That reminds me of an interesting case—a redheaded burlesque dancer who wanted to lose weight in her boobs—

            VANESSA
(Interrupting) Actually, that brings up an item I wanted to discuss.

            DR. ZIGMOND
Go on, please.

            VANESSA
You've claimed in the past that you can use hypnosis to enlarge a woman's

breasts?

                    DR. ZIGMOND
     That is correct, Ms. Talbot.   I have found that hypnosis can have a profound
effect upon a woman's self-image, and with an expensive—I mean, extended program of
treatment, I can produce an actual physical expansion, without the aid of implants,
injections or stuffing the subject's bra with Kleenex when she isn't looking.

                    VANESSA
Frankly, I find that difficult to believe.

     (DR. ZIGMOND takes his feet off his desk and turns his chair to face VANESSA.
His manner becomes more animated and exuberant as he tries to persuade her.)

                    DR. ZIGMOND
     Never underestimate the power of suggestion, Ms. Talbot.   With my methods not
only is there a physical benefit, there is a greater mental and emotional benefit—an
infusion of confidence, a burgeoning of self-esteem, a sense of self-satisfaction that only
comes when a woman can look at herself in the mirror and say, "By golly, I've got a
fabulous set of Ta-Tas!"

                    VANESSA
     So—you're telling me that it's not so important that a woman actually has big
breasts, but rather that she believes she has big breasts, and acts accordingly?

                    DR. ZIGMOND
     And why not?   We all believe that an outward change to ourselves—cosmetics,
liposuction, implants, and such—can produce an inward change in our self-esteem and
personality.   Well, why not just make the inward change and save oneself the trouble?

                    VANESSA
You make a good point, Doctor.   However—

                    DR. ZIGMOND
You're still skeptical?

                    VANESSA
To put it mildly—yes.

                    DR. ZIGMOND
Then there's only one way to convince you.

                    VANESSA
How is that?

                    DR. ZIGMOND
A demonstration. You must allow me to hypnotize you.

                    VANESSA
(Skeptical) Do you really think you can hypnotize me?


                    DR. ZIGMOND
If you allow yourself to be hypnotized—then I can hypnotize you.   It's as simple
as that.


                    VANESSA
I'm not so sure about this—


                    DR. ZIGMOND
Oh, you can trust me, Ms. Talbot.   After all—(Smiles and wiggles his
eyebrows)—I'm a doctor.


                    VANESSA
That's true, you are a doctor. (Pause) All right—what do I do?


                    DR. ZIGMOND
Why don't you join me on the couch?


          (They go over to the couch, and VANESSA takes a seat to Camera Right, while
DR. ZIGMOND takes the seat beside her at Camera Left, leaving a two-foot space
between them.)


                    DR. ZIGMOND
Now relax—close your eyes---take a deep breath—

(VANESSA closes her eyes and breathes in deeply---)

                    DR. ZIGMOND
And hold it for a count of one—two—three—four—five—exhale.

(VANESSA exhales, her eyes still closed.)

                    DR. ZIGMOND
Once again, a deep breath—

(VANESSA breathes in again)

                    DR. ZIGMOND
And again, hold it for one—two—three—four—five—exhale.

(VANESSA exhales again.)

                    DR. ZIGMOND

Splendid. Now keep breathing deeply.

(VANESSA breathes deeply, while DR. ZIGMOND checks the pockets of his lab coat.)

DR. ZIGMOND

Now—there are many methods of placing a subject in a hypnotic trance—but me? I'm a fan of the classics—

(From a pocket inside his lab coat he pulls out—you guessed it—a pocket watch. He swings the watch back and forth before VANESSA'S closed eyes.)

DR. ZIGMOND

Open your eyes, Ms. Talbot.

(VANESSA opens her eyes and spots the swinging watch.  Her eyes begin following it immediately.)

DR. ZIGMOND

That's it—just follow the watch with your eyes as it swings back and forth—back and forth—back—and forth—and as you breathe deeply—and your eyes follow the watch—you feel yourself become more and more relaxed—more and more relaxed—more—and more relaxed—

(VANESSA stares at the swinging watch and her eyelids start to droop lower and lower.)

DR. ZIGMOND

That's it—just let every part of your mind and body become deeply and completely relaxed---deeply and completely relaxed—Your eyes are getting heavier and heavier—it's so easy to just let your eyes close—let your eyes close—as you enter into deep---deep---deep hypnosis—

(As DR. ZIGMOND says the words, VANESSA'S eyes close again. Her shoulders slump a bit, but otherwise she remains upright, still breathing deeply.  DR. ZIGMOND puts the watch away and regards her for a moment as she sits hypnotized.)

DR. ZIGMOND

Now, my dear Ms. Talbot—may I call you Vanessa?

VANESSA

(Softly) Yes, Dr. Zigmond

DR. ZIGMOND

Vanessa, I want you to continue relaxing, to let yourself drift deeply and completely into deep, deep, hypnosis.  Let your mind become utterly blank, devoid of all thought, as you give your complete attention to my voice and only my voice.  Think

completely of nothing---completely of nothing---completely of nothing. (Pause)
Vanessa—what are you thinking about?

        VANESSA
(Still softly) Nothing.

        DR. ZIGMOND
Perfect.   Now, Vanessa—I want you to think about something.   I want you to
think about—your breasts.   I want you to think about how big and beautiful they are,
how round and firm they are, how magnificent and stupendous they are.   You have the
sexiest breasts of any woman you know, and more than a few you don't.   Vanessa, I want
you to repeat after me–"My breasts are simply the best."

        VANESSA
(Still softly) My breasts are simply the best.

        DR. ZIGMOND
Say it with a smile!

        VANESSA
(Smiling, in a normal tone) My breasts are simply the best.

        DR. ZIGMOND
Now, Vanessa—I want you to feel your breasts—feel how big and beautiful they
are, how round and firm they are, how magnificent and stupendous they are.   Let your
hands move to your breasts of their own accord, and let yourself feel for yourself your
magnificent, stupendous breasts.

        (VANESSA'S hands slowly move to her breasts and fondles her breasts through
her clothes, one in each hand.   She moans softly as she feels the pleasure of her
stimulation.)

        DR. ZIGMOND
You know, Vanessa—you could feel your magnificent and stupendous breasts
even better if your clothes weren't in the way.

        (VANESSA responds to his suggestion—first she takes off her suit jacket, then
opens her top to fondle her breasts through her bra.   DR. ZIGMOND smiles to see her
comply so well.)

        DR. ZIGMOND
Now—continue to remove your clothes as you repeat over and again—"My
breasts are simply the best—" feeling yourself becoming more aroused as you feel
yourself up.

        (VANESSA removes her top, then her bra. The Camera Pans Right and focuses on her as she continues playing with her breasts, caressing and fondling them over and under,   pulling and squeezing her nipples, her arousal growing with each moment.)

                    VANESSA
          My breasts are simply the best---My breasts are simply the
best—mmmmhmm—My breasts are simply the best---My breasts are simply the best—

          (VANESSA keeps repeating the words until DR. ZIGMOND enters the scene from Camera Left.   He has removed his lab coat and unzipped his fly, and now his enormous dick is hanging out for VANESSA to see—or would see, if her eyes were open. The Camera is at VANESSA'S eye level, with DR. ZIGMOND visible from the waist down.   We hear him in Voice-Over as he speaks to VANESSA.)

                    DR. ZIGMOND
          That's enough, Vanessa—now open your eyes, and fixate on what is in front of
you.

          (VANESSA opens her eyes, and fixates on DR. ZIGMOND'S cock. Her eyes widen as the Doctor's huge instrument completely fascinates her.   He starts waving it back and forth as she stares at and listens to his suggestions.)

                    DR. ZIGMOND
          (Voice-Over) Concentrate on my cock, Vanessa—follow it with your eyes as it swings back and forth—back and forth—back—and forth.   Isn't it big and beautiful? Isn't it strong, hard and powerful?   Isn't it stupendous and magnificent?

                    VANESSA
          Yes, Dr. Zigmond—oh, yes.

                    DR. ZIGMOND
          (Voice-Over) My cock is hypnotizing you, Vanessa.   My cock—is your master.

                    VANESSA
          Your—your cock is my master.

                    DR. ZIGMOND
          You will serve my cock, Vanessa.   You will obey my cock.

                    VANESSA
          I will obey your cock.   Your cock is my master.

                    DR. ZIGMOND
          My cock wants you to take it into your mouth—and suck on it—

          (VANESSA obeys, taking his cock into her mouth, using her lips and tongue alone while she places her hands on DR. ZIGMOND'S hips. We watch her enthusiastically fellate him for a few moments, then we Dissolve To the same scene, but now DR. ZIGMOND is nude and sitting on the couch, while VANESSA, completely undressed except for a garter belt, stockings, and high heels, is continuing her enthusiastic blowjob; she then moves to envelop his cock with her breasts and massage him Russian style. She smiles up at him as she does this, and he smiles back.)

                    VANESSA
          Dr. Zigmond—my breasts are simply the best.

                    DR. ZIGMOND
          Don't I know it, baby!   And how do you feel about my cock?

                    VANESSA
          Your cock is my master.

                    DR. ZIGMOND
          Well, your master wants to get inside of you, baby.

                    VANESSA
          Then I must obey.

          (VANESSA slides up DR. ZIGMOND'S body and sits on his lap, allowing his cock to slide into her pussy. They fuck in that way and in a number of other positions, first on the couch, then on the floor, before DR. ZIGMOND finishes all over her face and bust. Then the phone rings, and DR. ZIGMOND goes over to the desk and answers it.)

                    DR. ZIGMOND
          Yes?   (Pause) Henry Styles called?   (Another pause) A porn emergency?   Those are the worst!   (One more pause) All right—get the address, and tell him I'll be over as soon as I can.

          (He sets the phone on the desk without hanging it up. He goes over to VANESSA, who lies on the floor still deeply hypnotized.)

                    DR. ZIGMOND
          Vanessa, would you rise and stand before me?

          (VANESSA gets to her feet and stands before DR. ZIGMOND with a sweet, obedient smile on her face.)

                    DR. ZIGMOND
          My cock and myself want you to go lie down on the couch and fall into a deep, hypnotic sleep.   You will not awaken until I return, and then I will demonstrate further the power of hypnosis over your mind and body.   Do you understand?

                    VANESSA

Yes, Dr. Zigmond. (She bends over and speaks to his cock.) Yes, Master. (She straightens up to look at DR. ZIGMOND again.)

                    DR. ZIGMOND
And should you hear the words, "Your breasts are simply the best," you will return to this deep state of hypnotized bliss, and be ready to obey—and satisfy—whoever says them to you.

                    VANESSA
I will, Dr. Zigmond.

        (As VANESSA goes over to lie upon the couch, DR. ZIGMOND gathers his clothes.  He exits Camera Right, and we focus on VANESSA lying on the couch, as we Zoom In on her sleeping face.   Cut To a Close-Up of the phone off its hook on the desk. Cut To—)

INTERIOR—OFFICE LOBBY---DAY

        (HEATHER listens on the phone the DR. ZIGMOND forgot to hang up.   She smiles at what she's overheard.)

                    HEATHER
"Your breasts are simply the best"—I'll have to remember that.

        (She hangs up just as DR. ZIGMOND, fully dressed, enters the lobby and stops at HEATHER'S desk.   She hands him a slip of paper.)

                    HEATHER
Here's the address, Doctor.

                    DR. ZIGMOND
(Takes the paper and looks at it) All right—I'll be back in a little while, if the traffic isn't too bad.   Make sure Ms. Talbot doesn't leave, okay?

                    HEATHER
Don't worry, Doctor.   I'll pay careful attention to her.

                    DR. ZIGMOND
Good.   Talk to you later.

        (He exits the scene, and the Camera focuses on HEATHER, who smiles wide and hungry.)

                    HEATHER
Oh, baby, will I pay careful attention to her.

(The Camera lingers on her smile and the gleam in her eye.  Cut To—)
INTERIOR—PORN MOVIE STUDIO—DAY

(Two thoroughly gorgeous porn stars in skimpy lingerie, LACEY LOVING and
REBECCA DEE, are trying angrily to get at each other; they claw the air between them
as the notorious porn director HENRY STYLES and his faithful, yet slightly dim
assistant ERNIE try to keep them apart. The studio set has a large mattress set in the
middle, with several throw pillows thrown around it, and there are sheer curtains draped
in the background.  LACEY and REBECCA scream at each other as we join the debacle
already in progress—)

LACEY
Just wait 'til I get my hands on you, you bitch!

REBECCA
Don't call me a bitch, you bitch!   I'll bitch your ass all the way back to bitchland!

LACEY
You're the bitch who's getting bitched, you bitch!   How bad do you want it!

REBECCA
You're the bitch who's gonna get it, you bitching bitch!

HENRY
(Holding back LACEY) Dammit, don't you two know any other curse words?

LACEY
Let me go so I can give this bitch the bitch whupping she deserves!

ERNIE
(Holding back REBECCA) I don't think they know any other curse wor—

HENRY
(Interrupting) SHUT UP!   All of you, SHUT UP!

(Cut To a Reverse-Angle Shot of the studio.  A video camera on a tripod stands
alone as DR. ZIGMOND enters the scene and stands next to it.)

DR. ZIGMOND
Did I come at a bad time?

(Cut back To HENRY, LACEY, REBECCA and ERNIE. HENRY sees DR.
ZIGMOND Off-Camera, and breathes a sigh of relief.)

HENRY
Thank God you're here!   (To ERNIE) Take over!

(HENRY lets go of LACEY, and ERNIE quickly moves between the two angry porn stars; now they're clawing at him instead of the empty air.   Cut To DR. ZIGMOND as HENRY joins him next to the video camera.)

                    HENRY
They've been at it for the past hour!   I can't imagine where they get the energy!

(DR. ZIGMOND looks at HENRY and arches an eyebrow.)

                    HENRY
Don't look at me like that!   I don't supply my girls with drugs!   (Turns away) Not since my supplier got busted three weeks ago, anyway—

(Cut To LACEY, ERNIE and REBECCA as the struggle continues, with ERNIE looking much the worse for wear.)

                    ERNIE
Little—little help here, boss?

(Cut To HENRY and DR. ZIGMOND.)

                    HENRY
Can you do anything?

                    DR. ZIGMOND
You could always do a catfight video.

                    HENRY
(Indignant) Are you saying that I, the great Henry Styles, should stoop to doing catfight material?   I'm not some two-bit fly-by-night fetish mill!   I—am an artist!

                    DR. ZIGMOND
Well, you better be an artist who can pay my bill.

(DR. ZIGMOND exits the shot, and we Cut To LACEY, ERNIE and REBECCA again as DR. ZIGMOND enters the shot.   He claps his hands for attention as he says his line.)

                    DR. ZIGMOND
Ladies—ladies—LADIES!

(LACEY and REBECCA stop fighting and look at DR. ZIGMOND.   ERNIE staggers out from between them, and claps his hand on DR. ZIGMOND'S shoulder.)

                    ERNIE

Thanks, dude.
(ERNIE staggers out of the shot, and DR. ZIGMOND steps in between the two porn stars, who, drawn to his good looks and hypnotic presence, stop fighting long enough to catch their breath.   DR. ZIGMOND turns to LACEY and extends his hand.)

DR. ZIGMOND
Lacey Loving, isn't it?   A pleasure to meet you.   I'm Dr. Zigmond.

(LACEY takes his hand and shakes it.)

LACEY
Pleased to meet you too, Doctor.

(DR. ZIGMOND turns to REBECCA, extending his hand to her.)

DR. ZIGMOND
Rebecca Dee—a pleasure to see you again.   Tell me, does cum still taste like strawberry ice cream to you?

REBECCA
Not as much as it used to, Doctor.

DR. ZIGMOND
You should make an appointment with my office for a refresher session.   But tell me—what seems to be the problem here?

REBECCA
(Glaring angrily at LACEY) Nothing that can't be solved by HER tripping in front of a moving train!

LACEY
(Glaring angrily at REBECCA) Nothing that can't be solved by HER drinking a 40-ounce bottle of acid!

REBECCA
BITCH!

LACEY
BITCH!

(They attempt to launch themselves at each other, but DR. ZIGMOND in between them spreads his arms, effectively keeping them apart. They stop and pay attention as he speaks.)

DR. ZIGMOND
Ladies, please—all this fighting and hatred and negativity—doesn't it make you

just exhausted?  So very tired, so very exhausted— don't you just want to stop a moment and relax?  Relax and let everything go—

(From out of the pockets of his lab coat DR. ZIGMOND produces a cigarette lighter.  He ignites it, and it produces a long, bright, steady flame.  Cut To HENRY and ERNIE as they stand by the video camera.)

ERNIE
Hey—there's no smoking indoors—

HENRY
(Hissing) Shut up!

(Cut To LACEY, DR. ZIGMOND, and REBECCA, who take no notice of the other conversation as the two women fixate on the flame and DR. ZIGMOND continues speaking.)

DR. ZIGMOND
Now some people speak of raging, roaring flames—but as you can see, there is nothing roaring or raging about this flame.  It is calm—tranquil—and seeing it makes you feel calm—and tranquil.  And as you gaze upon the flame, let yourselves feel calm—and tranquil—and let your minds and bodies become more and more relaxed---more and more relaxed---more and more relaxed—

(LACEY and REBECCA stare at the flame.  Their eyelids droop and their arms hang limp at their sides. They continue to relax as DR. ZIGMOND continues.)

DR. ZIGMOND
Just let yourselves become just as calm and tranquil as the flame as you become more and more relaxed—and as you become so deeply and completely relaxed—as your minds become so deeply calm and tranquil—just let your eyes close—let your eyes close—and let yourselves become deeply and completely hypnotized---deeply and completely hypnotized---deeply and completely hypnotized—

(LACEY and REBECCA let their eyes close, and they stand beside DR. ZIGMOND deep in hypnosis. He puts the lighter away and stands admiring his handiwork.)

DR. ZIGMOND
(To LACEY) Lacey, is your hypnotized mind willing to accept my suggestions?

LACEY
Yes, Dr. Zigmond.

DR. ZIGMOND
(To REBECCA) Rebecca, is your hypnotized mind willing to accept my

suggestions?

                    REBECCA
Yes, Dr. Zigmond.


                    DR. ZIGMOND
Scrumptious.   Now Lacey—Rebecca—listen carefully, and respond willingly and completely to my suggestions.   In a moment I will snap my fingers—and when you hear me snap my fingers, you will open your eyes and see a person standing before you.   You will not recognize that person—you will not know who that person is—but you will see that the person is the sexiest, most beautiful person you have ever met, and you will become irresistibly aroused by the sight of that person. You want to have sex with that person—and you will have sex with that person, and anyone else who asks you today. Do you understand?


                    LACEY, REBECCA
(Together) Yes, Dr. Zigmond.


                    DR. ZIGMOND
(Smiling) Exquisite.


(He turns LACEY and REBECCA so they face each other, then exits the shot. Cut To HENRY and ERNIE standing by the video camera as DR. ZIGMOND enters the shot and stands by them.   He smiles at them, then snaps his fingers.   Cut To LACEY and REBECCA, whose eyes flutter open, then they look at each other and smile broadly. They embrace each other and kiss passionately, their raging argument forgotten.   They get on their knees and resume kissing, undressing each other as they make out. Cut To DR. ZIGMOND, HENRY and ERNIE as they stand and watch the action.)


                    ERNIE
(Stunned) Look at 'em go.


                    DR. ZIGMOND
Marvelous, isn't it?   That's the great thing about hypnosis and porn stars.   A hypnotized person will not, under normal circumstances, do anything they wouldn't usually do when awake.   But think about it—is there anything a porn star wouldn't do?


(Cut To LACEY and REBECCA, who are now intertwined on the mattress in the throes of lesbian passion.   Cut To DR. ZIGMOND, HENRY and ERNIE, who continue watching.)


                    DR. ZIGMOND
I must get back to the office.   You'll have my bill tomorrow morning, Henry.


(DR. ZIGMOND exits the scene.   HENRY turns and says his line while ERNIE rests his arm on the video camera.)

HENRY
You're worth every penny, Doc.   Thanks---

(He turns to watch the action again, and suddenly HENRY'S eyes widen in shock.)

HENRY
FUCK! I should be filming this!

(He slaps at ERNIE to shoo him off the camera.)

HENRY
Get off that thing, you dumb fuck!   Get off it!

ERNIE
Oww!  Hey!

(ERNIE backs away from the camera, and HENRY takes it and starts filming the action. Cut To LACEY and REBECCA still going at it hard and heavy. We focus on the action for some long, wonderful moments before we Cut To HENRY and ERNIE again; HENRY recording the action on video, while ERNIE absent-mindedly enjoys a bag of corn chips.)

HENRY
This is great stuff, great stuff!   Go get Frankie and Johnny, and have them join the action!

ERNIE
They left. (Munches a corn chip.)

(HENRY looks up from the camera at ERNIE.)

HENRY
They left?   What do you mean they left?

ERNIE
Well, the fight started, and they figured there wasn't going to be any action, so—

HENRY
WHY didn't you tell me!

ERNIE
Well, the fight started, and we were busy trying to bust them up—

(With a snarl, HENRY slaps the corn chips out of ERNIE'S hand.   Then he starts taking off his clothes as fast as he can, saying his line as he does so.)

                    HENRY
     There's only one thing to do—You film the action!   I'm going in!

     (ERNIE looks at the female stars Off-Camera, then looks back at HENRY.)

                    ERNIE
     I could go in. Can't I go in?

     (Now undressed, HENRY puts his hand on ERNIE'S shoulder.)

                    HENRY
     Listen to me, Ernie.   This is your moment—this is your time!   Any stupid guy
can be a stupid porn stud—but you, Ernie—you can be a director!   This is your big
chance, and I'm giving it to you!   You can do it!   I've taught you everything I know—

                    ERNIE
     (Interrupting) No you haven't.

                    HENRY
     (Continues as though uninterrupted)—And now it's up to you.   Make me proud!

     (HENRY exits the shot, leaving ERNIE alone with the video camera.   ERNIE
stands there with a look of profound disappointment on his face.)

                    ERNIE
     I can be a stupid porn stud.   I'm a stupid guy.

     (Cut To LACEY and REBECCA writhing about on the bed as HENRY enters the
shot. They take notice of him as he turns to yell at ERNIE Off-Camera.)

                    HENRY
     Just film the goddam scene!

     (He turns to the women with a smooth, sugary smile.)

                    HENRY
     Hello, girls—shall we dance?

     (LACEY and REBECCA pull the naked HENRY down on the bed and start
pleasuring him.   They suck and fuck him just as passionately as they did each other
moments before.   When HENRY finally finishes, he's so exhausted he passes out.   Cut
To ERNIE, who realizes his opportunity and goes over to the girls, who look at him and
smile.)

                    ERNIE

I want to go in too.

(LACEY and REBECCA leave the unconscious HENRY on the bed, and stand up to caress ERNIE and press close to him and play with his hair.  He looks at the camera, smiles and gives the "thumbs up."  Dissolve To—)

INTERIOR–TREATMENT ROOM TWO–DAY

(BRENT and APHRODITE are still sitting on the love seat; BRENT is happily exhausted, while APHRODITE, her eyes closed, plays with her breasts.  A moment later, her eyes flutter open, and she's awake—and she's LISA again.)

    LISA
Wow—that was something else.   (To BRENT) Hi, I'm Lisa.

    BRENT
Umm—I'm Brent.

    LISA
(Shakes his hand and smiles) Pleased to meet you, Brent.

    BRENT
I thought your name was Aphrodite.

    LISA
Oh, that was just me being hypnotized.

    BRENT
Oh—okay. (Pause) What's that like?

    LISA
Well—it's like I'm dreaming, but I'm awake at the same time.   It's like I'm myself, but I'm also someone else. And it just makes perfect sense that I should do whatever the Doctor tells me to do. That's not too weird, is it?

    BRENT
Not at all.   I think you're really great when you're hypnotized.

    LISA
(Chuckles) Thank you.

(From Off-Camera we hear a knock at the door.)

    LISA
I'll get that—it could be the Doctor.

(BRENT pulls on his pants while LISA quickly slips on her toga and goes to open

the door.   As it turns out, JERRY is on the other side.)
                    JERRY
Uh—hello there.


          LISA
Hello—I thought you were the Doctor.


          JERRY
I was looking for him myself.   You don't know where he is?


          LISA
I'm afraid not.   (Extends her hand) I'm Lisa, by the way.


          JERRY
(Shakes her hand) Hi, Lisa.   I'm Jerry.   Really nice to meet you.


          LISA
Come on in.


     (JERRY enters the room and closes the door behind him.   BRENT comes to stand
by LISA, the vanity mirror in his hand.)


          JERRY
So—why are you here?


          LISA
Well, Dr. Zigmond said he could help me enjoy anal sex, so I---


          BRENT
(Interrupting) Excuse me, but is this your mirror?


     (LISA turns to BRENT and takes the mirror.   She says her line as she looks into
the mirror.)


          LISA
I didn't bring a mirror with me—this is a really nice one—though---


     (Her voice trails off as she brings the mirror up to eye level.   She stares into it,
thoroughly absorbed in her reflection.   She becomes oblivious to JERRY and BRENT as
she once again drops into trance.)


          JERRY
Lisa?   Lisa, are you okay?   (To BRENT) What's going on?


          BRENT
She was like this when I came in.   Here, let me try something.   (To LISA) One,

two—three.
(LISA blinks slowly, and then arches her back, becoming APHRODITE again.
She smiles at each of the men, reaching to caress them with her hands.)

                    APHRODITE
I am Aphrodite, the goddess of love.   What may I do to satisfy you both?

(JERRY and BRENT look at each other and smile.)

                    JERRY
This day just keeps getting better and better!

(Dissolve to JERRY, BRENT and APHRODITE all nude and on the floor as
JERRY and BRENT fuck APHRODITE, and she fucks them back.   JERRY and BRENT
take turns being sucked by her while the other fucks her pussy, and there even may be
some double penetration. Finally they come all over her face and breasts, and ths scene
ends with JERRY and BRENT lying on the floor exhausted, while APHRODITE kneels
over them, smiling down benevolently at her subjects.   Dissolve To—)

INTERIOR—DR. ZIGMOND'S OFFICE—DAY

(The nude VANESSA TALBOT slowly awakens from hypnotized sleep.   She
moans, her eyes flutter open, and she sits up on the couch.)

                    VANESSA
What—what happened?   How did I—where are my—?

(She looks down at herself and realizes with a shock she's undressed.)

                    VANESSA
(Frantically) Where are my clothes?   Oh my God, where are my clothes?   What
did that son-of-a-bitch do to me?   What did he do to me?

                    HEATHER
(Voice-Over) Offhand, I'd say he hypnotized you and had his way with you—

(VANESSA looks to Camera Right, and we Cut To HEATHER standing in the
open doorway of DR. ZIGMOND'S office.)

                    HEATHER
(Smiling) But it looks to me like you both had a really good time.

(VANESSA begins gathering up her clothes as HEATHER enters, closing the door
behind her.   Having gathered her clothes, she stands before HEATHER, holding her
bundle of clothes before her with both hands as she angrily confronts HEATHER.)

                    VANESSA
     You just wait!   When I'm finished with my article, Dr. Zigmond will be lucky if
he doesn't spend the rest of his life in jail!   I'll expose him for the patient-molesting
fraud he truly is!   And you'll be locked up as well for being an accessory to his crimes!

                    HEATHER
     Can I say just one thing before you bring the cops down about our heads?
Something that will allow you to see this in a different light?

                    VANESSA
     You actually think you can change my mind?   What can you possibly say to do
that?

                    HEATHER
     Your breasts—are simply the best.

     (VANESSA stands still for a moment.   Her face slackens, and the energy drains
from her all at once. Her arms go limp, and we Cut To a Close-Up shot of her clothes
hitting the floor.   Cut To VANESSA, once again deep in trance, and HEATHER,
standing and smiling wide.)

                    HEATHER
     Have a seat, darling.

     (VANESSA sits on the couch again, and HEATHER sits beside her. VANESSA
stares blankly ahead as HEATHER fondles VANESSA'S bare breasts.)


                    VANESSA
     I'm hypnotized again, aren't I?

                    HEATHER
     Yes—you're hypnotized again—

     (She gently touches VANESSA'S cheek, turning her head to face her.)

                    HEATHER
     But you know you love it, baby.

     (HEATHER kisses VANESSA full on the lips, and she returns the passion.   Soon
HEATHER is naked as well, and they kiss, lick, suck and hump their way through the rest
of the scene.   When they're finished, HEATHER lies on top of VANESSA, looking into
her eyes.)

                    HEATHER
    Listen to me, Vanessa.   Dr. Zigmond will be back soon—and when he asks you
what you're going to write in your article, this is what you're going to say—

    (Cut To—)

INTERIOR–OFFICE LOBBY—DAY

    (HEATHER, fully dressed, stands behind her desk smiling as VANESSA, fully
dressed and awake, stands in front of the desk and says goodbye to DR. ZIGMOND, who
has returned from the studio.)

                    VANESSA
    (Smiling) I had quite an enlightening time today, Dr. Zigmond.   I'll certainly
recommend you to all my readers as the man to go to for anyone wishing to deeply
explore their sexuality.

                    DR. ZIGMOND
    Thank you, Ms. Talbot.   And if you should ever feel the need for a personal
hypnotic consultation—there'll be no charge.

                    VANESSA
    Thank you, Doctor.   I may just take you up on that.

                    DR. ZIGMOND
    I'll look forward to it.   Good day, Ms. Talbot.

                    VANESSA
    Good day to you too, Doctor.

    (VANESSA exits the scene, and DR. ZIGMOND goes to stand by HEATHER.)

                    DR. ZIGMOND
    A most rewarding day, wasn't it, HEATHER?

                    HEATHER
    Yes, but it was a long day, too. I'll be glad to get home—I'm so tired.


    (Dr. ZIGMOND puts his hand gently on HEATHER'S chin, and turns her head to
face him. HEATHER stares into DR. ZIGMOND'S eyes, and her arms slowly drop to her
sides as her face goes blank.)

                    DR. ZIGMOND
    Yes, Heather—you are feeling tired.   Tired, and sleepy.   You just want to

relax—let your mind and body relax—

    (DR. ZIGMOND snaps his fingers, and HEATHER stands completely still, deep in trance. She turns her head to face forward, and stares blankly into space.)

           DR. ZIGMOND
You'd like to come home with me tonight, wouldn't you, Heather?

           HEATHER
Yes, Dr. Zigmond.

           DR. ZIGMOND
Wonderful.   Then go wait for me in my car, and I'll join you shortly.

           HEATHER
As you command, Dr. Zigmond.

    (HEATHER walks out from behind the desk, and exits the scene.   DR. ZIGMOND watches her as she walks away.   He smiles and faces the Camera.)

           DR. ZIGMOND
I love my job.

    (He exits the scene, following HEATHER'S route—and we Fade To Black.)

**THE END**

**ROLL CLOSING CREDITS**

**FADE OUT**